George Cruikshank

William Makepeace Thackeray

George Cruikshank

Table of Contents

George Cruikshank

William Makepeace Thackeray

Accusations of ingratitude, and just accusations no doubt, are made against every inhabitant of this wicked world, and the fact is, that a man who is ceaselessly engaged in its trouble and turmoil, borne hither and thither upon the fierce waves of the crowd, bustling, shifting, struggling to keep himself somewhat above water—fighting for reputation, or more likely for bread, and ceaselessly occupied to–day with plans for appeasing the eternal appetite of inevitable hunger to–morrow—a man in such straits has hardly time to think of anything but himself, and, as in a sinking ship, must make his own rush for the boats, and fight, struggle, and trample for safety. In the midst of such a combat as this, the "ingenious arts, which prevent the ferocity of the manners, and act upon them as an emollient" (as the philosophic bard remarks in the Latin Grammar) are likely to be jostled to death, and then forgotten. The world will allow no such compromises between it and that which does not belong to it—no two gods must we serve; but (as one has seen in some old portraits) the horrible glazed eyes of Necessity are always fixed upon you; fly away as you will, black Care sits behind you, and with his ceaseless gloomy croaking drowns the voice of all more cheerful companions. Happy he whose fortune has placed him where there is calm and plenty, and who has the wisdom not to give up his quiet in quest of visionary gain.

Here is, no doubt, the reason why a man, after the period of his boyhood, or first youth, makes so few friends. Want and ambition (new acquaintances which are introduced to him along with his beard) thrust away all other society from him. Some old friends remain, it is true, but these are become as a habit—a part of your selfishness; and, for new ones, they are selfish as you are. Neither member of the new partnership has the capital of affection and kindly feeling, or can even afford the time that is requisite for the establishment of the new firm. Damp and chill the shades of the prison–house begin to close round us, and that "vision splendid" which has accompanied our steps in our journey daily farther from the east, fades away and dies into the light of common day.

And what a common day! what a foggy, dull, shivering apology for light is this kind of muddy twilight through which we are about to tramp and flounder for the rest of our existence, wandering farther and farther from the beauty and freshness and from the kindly gushing springs of clear gladness that made all around us green in our youth! One wanders and gropes in a slough of stock–jobbing, one sinks or rises in a storm of politics, and in either case it is as good to fall as to rise—to mount a bubble on the crest of the wave, as to sink a stone to the bottom.

The reader who has seen the name affixed to the head of this article scarcely expected to be entertained with a declamation upon ingratitude, youth, and the vanity of human pursuits, which may seem at first sight to have little to do with the subject in hand. But (although we reserve the privilege of discoursing upon whatever subject shall suit us, and by no means admit the public has any right to ask in our sentences for any meaning, or any connection whatever) it happens that, in this particular instance, there is an undoubted connection. In Susan's case, as recorded by Wordsworth, what connection had the corner of Wood Street with a mountain ascending, a vision of trees, and a nest by the Dove? Why should the song of a thrush cause bright volumes of vapor to glide through Lothbury, and a river to flow on through the vale of Cheapside? As she stood at that corner of Wood Street, a mop and a pail in her hand most likely, she heard the bird singing, and straight–way began pining and yearning for the days of her youth, forgetting the proper business of the pail and mop. Even so we are moved by the sight of some of Mr. Cruikshank's works—the "Busen fuhlt sich jugendlich erschuttert," the "schwankende Gestalten" of youth flit before one again,—Cruikshank's thrush begins to pipe and carol, as in the days of boyhood; hence misty moralities, reflections, and sad and pleasant remembrances arise. He is the friend of the young especially. Have we not read, all the story–books that his wonderful pencil has illustrated? Did we not forego tarts, in order to buy his "Breaking–up," or his "Fashionable Monstrosities" of the year eighteen hundred and something? Have we not before us, at this very moment, a print,—one of the admirable "Illustrations of Phrenology"—which entire work was purchased by a joint–stock company of boys, each drawing lots afterwards for the separate prints, and taking his choice in rotation? The writer of this, too, had the honor of drawing the first lot, and seized immediately upon "Philoprogenitiveness"—a marvellous print (our copy is not at all improved by being colored, which operation we performed on it ourselves)—a marvellous print, indeed,—full of ingenuity and fine jovial humor. A father, possessor of an enormous nose and family, is surrounded by the latter, who are, some of them, embracing the former. The composition writhes and twists about like the Kermes of Rubens. No less than seven little men and women in nightcaps, in frocks, in bibs, in breeches, are clambering about the head, knees, and arms of the man with the nose; their noses, too, are preternaturally developed—the twins in the cradle have noses of the most considerable kind. The second daughter, who is watching them; the youngest but two, who sits squalling in a certain wicker chair; the eldest son, who is yawning; the eldest daughter, who is preparing with the gravy of two mutton–chops a savory dish of Yorkshire pudding for eighteen persons; the youths who are examining her operations (one a literary gentleman, in a remarkably neat nightcap and pinafore, who has just had his finger in the pudding); the genius who is at work on the slate, and the two honest lads who are hugging the good–humored washerwoman, their mother,—all, all, save, this worthy woman, have noses of the largest size. Not handsome certainly are they, and yet everybody must be charmed with the picture. It is full of grotesque beauty. The artist has at the back of his own skull, we are certain, a huge bump of philoprogenitiveness. He loves children in his heart; every one of those he has drawn is perfectly happy, and jovial, and affectionate, and innocent as possible. He makes them with large noses, but he loves them, and you always find something kind in the midst of his humor, and the ugliness redeemed by a sly touch of beauty. The smiling mother reconciles one with all the hideous family: they have all something of the mother in them—something kind, and generous, and tender.

Knight's, in Sweeting's Alley; Fairburn's, in a court off Ludgate Hill; Hone's, in Fleet Street—bright, enchanted palaces, which George Cruikshank used to people with grinning, fantastical imps, and merry, harmless sprites,—where are they? Fairburn's shop knows him no more; not only has Knight disappeared from Sweeting's Alley, but, as we are given to understand, Sweetings Alley has disappeared from the face of the globe. Slop, the atrocious Castlereagh, the sainted Caroline (in a tight pelisse, with feathers in her head), the "Dandy of sixty," who used to glance at us from Hone's friendly windows—where are they? Mr. Cruikshank may have drawn a thousand better things since the days when these were; but they are to us a thousand times more pleasing than anything else he has done. How we used to believe in them! to stray miles out of the way on holidays, in order to ponder for an hour before that delightful window in Sweeting's Alley! in walks through Fleet Street, to vanish abruptly down Fairburn's passage, and there make one at his "charming gratis" exhibition. There used to be a crowd round the window in those days, of grinning, good–natured mechanics, who spelt the songs, and spoke them out for the benefit of the company, and who received the points of humor with a general sympathizing roar. Where are these people now? You never hear any laughing at HB.; his pictures are a great deal too genteel for that—polite points of wit, which strike one as exceedingly clever and pretty, and cause one to smile in a quiet, gentleman–like kind of way.

There must be no smiling with Cruikshank. A man who does not laugh outright is a dullard, and has no heart; even the old dandy of sixty must have laughed at his own wondrous grotesque image, as they say Louis Philippe did, who saw all the caricatures that were made of himself. And there are some of Cruikshank's designs which have the blessed faculty of creating laughter as often as you see them. As Diggory says in the play, who is bidden by his master not to laugh while waiting at table—"Don't tell the story of Grouse in the Gun– room, master, or I can't help laughing." Repeat that history ever so often, and at the proper moment, honest Diggory is sure to explode. Every man, no doubt, who loves Cruikshank has his "Grouse in the Gun–room." There is a fellow in the "Points of Humor" who is offering to eat up a certain little general, that has made us happy any time these sixteen years: his huge mouth is a perpetual well of laughter—buckets full of fun can be drawn from it. We have formed no such friendships as that boyish one of the man with the mouth. But though, in our eyes, Mr. Cruikshank reached his apogee some eighteen years since, it must not be imagined that such is really the case. Eighteen sets of children have since then learned to love and admire him, and may many more of their successors be brought up in the same delightful faith. It is not the artist who fails, but the men who grow cold—the men, from whom the illusions (why illusions? realities) of youth disappear one by one; who have no leisure to be happy, no blessed holidays, but only fresh cares at Midsummer and Christmas, being the inevitable seasons which bring us bills instead of pleasures. Tom, who comes bounding home from school, has the doctor's account in his trunk, and his father goes to sleep at the pantomime to which he takes him. Pater infelix, you too have laughed at clown, and the magic wand of spangled harlequin; what delightful enchantment did it wave around you, in the golden days "when George the Third was king!" But our clown lies in his grave; and our harlequin, Ellar, prince of how many enchanted islands, was he not at Bow Street the other day,* in his dirty, tattered, faded motley—seized as a law–breaker, for acting at a penny theatre, after having wellnigh starved in the streets, where nobody would listen to his old guitar? No one gave a shilling to bless him: not one of us who owe him so much.

4

George Cruikshank

* This was written in 1840.

We know not if Mr. Cruikshank will be very well pleased at finding his name in such company as that of Clown and Harlequin; but he, like them, is certainly the children's friend. His drawings abound in feeling for these little ones, and hideous as in the course of his duty he is from time to time compelled to design them, he never sketches one without a certain pity for it, and imparting to the figure a certain grotesque grace. In happy schoolboys he revels; plum–pudding and holidays his needle has engraved over and over again; there is a design in one of the comic almanacs of some young gentlemen who are employed in administering to a schoolfellow the correction of the pump, which is as graceful and elegant as a drawing of Stothard. Dull books about children George Cruikshank makes bright with illustrations—there is one published by the ingenious and opulent Mr. Tegg. It is entitled "Mirth and Morality," the mirth being, for the most part, on the side of the designer—the morality, unexceptionable certainly, the author's capital. Here are then, to these moralities, a smiling train of mirths supplied by George Cruikshank. See yonder little fellows butterfly–hunting across a common! Such a light, brisk, airy, gentleman–like drawing was never made upon such a theme. Who, cries the author—

```
"Who has not chased the butterfly,
   And crushed its slender legs and wings,
 And heaved a moralizing sigh:
   Alas! how frail are human things!"
```

A very unexceptionable morality truly; but it would have puzzled another than George Cruikshank to make mirth out of it as he has done. Away, surely not on the wings of these verses, Cruikshank's imagination begins to soar; and he makes us three darling little men on a green common, backed by old farmhouses, somewhere about May. A great mixture of blue and clouds in the air, a strong fresh breeze stirring, Tom's jacket flapping in the same, in order to bring down the insect queen or king of spring that is fluttering above him,—he renders all this with a few strokes on a little block of wood not two inches square, upon which one may gaze for hours, so merry and lifelike a scene does it present. What a charming creative power is this, what a privilege—to be a god, and create little worlds upon paper, and whole generations of smiling, jovial men, women, and children half inch high, whose portraits are carried abroad, and have the faculty of making us monsters of six feet curious and happy in our turn. Now, who would imagine that an artist could make anything of such a subject as this? The writer begins by stating,—

```
"I love to go back to the days of my youth,
    And to reckon my joys to the letter,
And to count o'er the friends that I have in the world,
    Ay, and those who are gone to a better."
```

This brings him to the consideration of his uncle. "Of all the men I have ever known," says he, "my uncle united the greatest degree of cheerfulness with the sobriety of manhood. Though a man when I was a boy, he was yet one of the most agreeable companions I ever possessed. . . . He embarked for America, and nearly twenty years passed by before he came back again; . . . but oh, how altered!—he was in every sense of the word an old man, his body and mind were enfeebled, and second childishness had come upon him. How often have I bent over him, vainly endeavoring to recall to his memory the scenes we had shared together: and how frequently, with an aching heart, have I gazed on his vacant and lustreless eye, while he has amused himself in clapping his hands and singing with a quavering voice a verse of a psalm." Alas! such are the consequences of long residences in America, and of old age even in uncles! Well, the point of this morality is, that the uncle one day in the morning of life vowed that he would catch his two nephews and tie them together, ay, and actually did so, for all the efforts the rogues made to run away from him; but he was so fatigued that he declared he never would make the attempt again, whereupon the nephew remarks,—"Often since then, when engaged in enterprises beyond my strength, have I called to mind the determination of my uncle."

Does it not seem impossible to make a picture out of this? And yet George Cruikshank has produced a charming design, in which the uncles and nephews are so prettily portrayed that one is reconciled to their existence, with all their moralities. Many more of the mirths in this little book are excellent, especially a great figure of a parson entering church on horseback,—an enormous parson truly, calm, unconscious, unwieldy. As Zeuxis had a bevy of virgins in order to make his famous picture—his express virgin—a clerical host must have passed under Cruikshank's eyes before he sketched this little, enormous parson of parsons.

Being on the subject of children's books, how shall we enough praise the delightful

6

George Cruikshank

German nursery-tales, and Cruikshank's illustrations of them? We coupled his name with pantomime awhile since, and sure never pantomimes were more charming than these. Of all the artists that ever drew, from Michael Angelo upwards and downwards, Cruikshank was the man to illustrate these tales, and give them just the proper admixture of the grotesque, the wonderful, and the graceful. May all Mother Bunch's collection be similarly indebted to him; may "Jack the Giant Killer," may "Tom Thumb," may "Puss in Boots," be one day revivified by his pencil. Is not Whittington sitting yet on Highgate hill, and poor Cinderella (in that sweetest of all fairy stories) still pining in her lonely chimney-nook? A man who has a true affection for these delightful companions of his youth is bound to be grateful to them if he can, and we pray Mr. Cruikshank to remember them.

It is folly to say that this or that kind of humor is too good for the public, that only a chosen few can relish it. The best humor that we know of has been as eagerly received by the public as by the most delicate connoisseur. There is hardly a man in England who can read but will laugh at Falstaff and the humor of Joseph Andrews; and honest Mr. Pickwick's story can be felt and loved by any person above the age of six. Some may have a keener enjoyment of it than others, but all the world can be merry over it, and is always ready to welcome it. The best criterion of good humor is success, and what a share of this has Mr. Cruikshank had! how many millions of mortals has he made happy! We have heard very profound persons talk philosophically of the marvellous and mysterious manner in which he has suited himself to the time—fait vibrer la fibre populaire (as Napoleon boasted of himself), supplied a peculiar want felt at a peculiar period, the simple secret of which is, as we take it, that he, living amongst the public, has with them a general wide-hearted sympathy, that he laughs at what they laugh at, that he has a kindly spirit of enjoyment, with not a morsel of mysticism in his composition; that he pities and loves the poor, and jokes at the follies of the great, and that he addresses all in a perfectly sincere and manly way. To be greatly successful as a professional humorist, as in any other calling, a man must be quite honest, and show that his heart is in his work. A bad preacher will get admiration and a hearing with this point in his favor, where a man of three times his acquirements will only find indifference and coldness. Is any man more remarkable than our artist for telling the truth after his own manner? Hogarth's honesty of purpose was as conspicuous in an earlier time, and we fancy that Gilray would have been far more successful and more powerful but for that unhappy bribe, which turned the whole course of his humor into an unnatural channel. Cruikshank would not for any bribe say what he did not think, or lend his aid to sneer down anything meritorious, or to praise any thing or person that deserved censure. When he levelled his wit against the Regent, and did his very prettiest for the Princess, he most certainly believed, along with the great body of the people whom he represents, that the Princess was the most spotless, pure−mannered darling of a Princess that ever married a heartless debauchee of a Prince Royal. Did not millions believe with him, and noble and learned lords take their oaths to her Royal Highness's innocence? Cruikshank would not stand by and see a woman ill−used, and so struck in for her rescue, he and the people belaboring with all their might the party who were making the attack, and determining, from pure sympathy and indignation, that the woman must be innocent because her husband treated her so foully.

To be sure we have never heard so much from Mr. Cruikshank's own lips, but any man who will examine these odd drawings, which first made him famous, will see what an honest hearty hatred the champion of woman has for all who abuse her, and will admire the energy with which he flings his wood−blocks at all who side against her. Canning, Castlereagh, Bexley, Sidmouth, he is at them, one and all; and as for the Prince, up to what a whipping−post of ridicule did he tie that unfortunate old man! And do not let squeamish Tories cry out about disloyalty; if the crown does wrong, the crown must be corrected by the nation, out of respect, of course, for the crown. In those days, and by those people who so bitterly attacked the son, no word was ever breathed against the father, simply because he was a good husband, and a sober, thrifty, pious, orderly man.

This attack upon the Prince Regent we believe to have been Mr. Cruikshank's only effort as a party politician. Some early manifestoes against Napoleon we find, it is true, done in the regular John Bull style, with the Gilray model for the little upstart Corsican: but as soon as the Emperor had yielded to stern fortune our artist's heart relented (as Beranger's did on the other side of the water), and many of our readers will doubtless recollect a fine drawing of "Louis XVIII. trying on Napoleon's boots," which did not certainly fit the gouty son of Saint Louis. Such satirical hits as these, however, must not be considered as political, or as anything more than the expression of the artist's national British idea of Frenchmen.

It must be confessed that for that great nation Mr. Cruikshank entertains a considerable contempt. Let the reader examine the "Life in Paris," or the five hundred designs in which Frenchmen are introduced, and he will find them almost invariably thin, with ludicrous spindle−shanks, pigtails, outstretched hands, shrugging shoulders, and queer hair and mustachios. He has the British idea of a Frenchman; and if he does not believe that the inhabitants of France are for the most part dancing–masters and barbers, yet takes care to depict such in preference, and would not speak too well of them. It is curious how these traditions endure. In France, at the present moment, the Englishman on the stage is the caricatured Englishman at the time of the war, with a shock red head, a long white coat, and invariable gaiters. Those who wish to study this subject should peruse Monsieur Paul de Kock's histories of "Lord Boulingrog" and "Lady Crockmilove." On the other hand, the old emigre has taken his station amongst us, and we doubt if a good British gallery would understand that such and such a character WAS a Frenchman unless he appeared in the ancient traditional costume.

A curious book, called "Life in Paris," published in 1822, contains a number of the artist's plates in the aquatint style; and though we believe he had never been in that capital, the designs have a great deal of life in them, and pass muster very well. A villanous race of shoulder–shrugging mortals are his Frenchmen indeed. And the heroes of the tale, a certain Mr. Dick Wildfire, Squire Jenkins, and Captain O'Shuffleton, are made to show the true British superiority on every occasion when Britons and French are brought together. This book was one among the many that the designer's genius has caused to be popular; the plates are not carefully executed, but, being colored, have a pleasant, lively look. The same style was adopted in the once famous book called "Tom and Jerry, or Life in London," which must have a word of notice here, for, although by no means Mr. Cruikshank's best work, his reputation was extraordinarily raised by it. Tom and Jerry were as popular twenty years since as Mr. Pickwick and Sam Weller now are; and often have we wished, while reading the biographies of the latter celebrated personages, that they had been described as well by Mr. Cruikshank's pencil as by Mr. Dickens's pen.

As for Tom and Jerry, to show the mutability of human affairs and the evanescent nature of reputation, we have been to the British Museum and no less than five circulating libraries in quest of the book, and "Life in London," alas, is not to be found at any one of them. We can only, therefore, speak of the work from recollection, but have still a very clear remembrance of the leather gaiters of Jerry Hawthorn, the green spectacles of Logic, and the hooked nose of Corinthian Tom. They were the schoolboy's delight; and in the days when the work appeared we firmly believed the three heroes above named to be types of the most elegant, fashionable young fellows the town afforded, and thought their occupations and amusements were those of all high–bred English gentlemen. Tom knocking down the watchman at Temple Bar; Tom and Jerry dancing at Almack's; or flirting in the saloon at the theatre; at the night– houses, after the play; at Tom Cribb's, examining the silver cup then in the possession of that champion; at the chambers of Bob Logic, who, seated at a cabinet piano, plays a waltz to which Corinthian Tom and Kate are dancing; ambling gallantly in Rotten Row; or examining the poor fellow at Newgate who was having his chains knocked off before hanging: all these scenes remain indelibly engraved upon the mind, and so far we are independent of all the circulating libraries in London.

As to the literary contents of the book, they have passed sheer away. It was, most likely, not particularly refined; nay, the chances are that it was absolutely vulgar. But it must have had some merit of its own, that is clear; it must have given striking descriptions of life in some part or other of London, for all London read it, and went to see it in its dramatic shape. The artist, it is said, wished to close the career of the three heroes by bringing them all to ruin, but the writer, or publishers, would not allow any such melancholy subjects to dash the merriment of the public, and we believe Tom, Jerry, and Logic, were married off at the end of the tale, as if they had been the most moral personages in the world. There is some goodness in this pity, which authors and the public are disposed to show towards certain agreeable, disreputable characters of romance. Who would mar the prospects of honest Roderick Random, or Charles Surface, or Tom Jones? only a very stern moralist indeed. And in regard of Jerry Hawthorn and that hero without a surname, Corinthian Tom, Mr. Cruikshank, we make little doubt, was glad in his heart that he was not allowed to have his own way.

Soon after the "Tom and Jerry" and the "Life in Paris," Mr. Cruikshank produced a much more elaborate set of prints, in a work which was called "Points of Humor." These "Points" were selected from various comic works, and did not, we believe, extend beyond a couple of numbers, containing about a score of copper–plates. The collector of humorous designs cannot fail to have them in his portfolio, for they contain some of the very best efforts of Mr. Cruikshank's genius, and though not quite so highly labored as some of his later productions, are none the worse, in our opinion, for their comparative want of finish. All the effects are perfectly given, and the expression is as good as it could be in the most delicate engraving upon steel. The artist's style, too, was then completely formed; and, for our parts, we should say that we preferred his manner of 1825 to any other which he has adopted since. The first picture, which is called "The Point of Honor," illustrates the old story of the officer who, on being accused of cowardice for refusing to fight a duel, came among his brother officers and flung a

George Cruikshank

lighted grenade down upon the floor, before which his comrades fled ignominiously. This design is capital, and the outward rush of heroes, walking, trampling, twisting, scuffling at the door, is in the best style of the grotesque. You see but the back of most of these gentlemen; into which, nevertheless, the artist has managed to throw an expression of ludicrous agony that one could scarcely have expected to find in such a part of the human figure. The next plate is not less good. It represents a couple who, having been found one night tipsy, and lying in the same gutter, were, by a charitable though misguided gentleman, supposed to be man and wife, and put comfortably to bed together. The morning came; fancy the surprise of this interesting pair when they awoke and discovered their situation. Fancy the manner, too, in which Cruikshank has depicted them, to which words cannot do justice. It is needless to state that this fortuitous and temporary union was followed by one more lasting and sentimental, and that these two worthy persons were married, and lived happily ever after.

We should like to go through every one of these prints. There is the jolly miller, who, returning home at night, calls upon his wife to get him a supper, and falls to upon rashers of bacon and ale. How he gormandizes, that jolly miller! rasher after rasher, how they pass away frizzling and, smoking from the gridiron down that immense grinning gulf of a mouth. Poor wife! how she pines and frets, at that untimely hour of midnight to be obliged to fry, fry, fry perpetually, and minister to the monster's appetite. And yonder in the clock: what agonized face is that we see? By heavens, it is the squire of the parish. What business has he there? Let us not ask. Suffice it to say, that he has, in the hurry of the moment, left up stairs his br———; his—psha! a part of his dress, in short, with a number of bank-notes in the pockets. Look in the next page, and you will see the ferocious, bacon-devouring ruffian of a miller is actually causing this garment to be carried through the village and cried by the town-crier. And we blush to be obliged to say that the demoralized miller never offered to return the banknotes, although he was so mighty scrupulous in endeavoring to find an owner for the corduroy portfolio in which he had found them.

Passing from this painful subject, we come, we regret to state, to a series of prints representing personages not a whit more moral. Burns's famous "Jolly Beggars" have all had their portraits drawn by Cruikshank. There is the lovely "hempen widow," quite as interesting and romantic as the famous Mrs. Sheppard, who has at the lamented demise of her husband adopted the very same consolation.

George Cruikshank

```
"My curse upon them every one,
 They've hanged my braw John Highlandman;


        .       .       .       .


 And now a widow I must mourn
 Departed joys that ne'er return;
 No comfort but a hearty can
 When I think on John Highlandman."
```

Sweet "raucle carlin," she has none of the sentimentality of the English highwayman's lady; but being wooed by a tinker and

```
"A pigmy scraper wi' his fiddle
 Wha us'd to trystes and fairs to driddle,"
```

prefers the practical to the merely musical man. The tinker sings with a noble candor, worthy of a fellow of his strength of body and station in life—

```
"My bonnie lass, I work in brass,
   A tinker is my station;
 I've travell'd round all Christian ground
   In this my occupation.
 I've ta'en the gold, I've been enroll'd
   In many a noble squadron;
 But vain they search'd when off I march'd
   To go an' clout the caudron."
```

It was his ruling passion. What was military glory to him, forsooth? He had the greatest contempt for it, and loved freedom and his copper kettle a thousand times better—a kind of hardware Diogenes. Of fiddling he has no better opinion. The picture represents the "sturdy caird" taking "poor gut-scraper" by the beard,—drawing his "roosty rapier," and swearing to "speet him like a pliver" unless he would relinquish the bonnie lassie for ever—

```
"Wi' ghastly ee, poor tweedle-dee
   Upon his hunkers bended,
 An' pray'd for grace wi' ruefu' face,
   An' so the quarrel ended."
```

George Cruikshank

Hark how the tinker apostrophizes the violinist, stating to the widow at the same time the advantages which she might expect from an alliance with himself:—

```
"Despise that shrimp, that withered imp,
   Wi' a' his noise and caperin';
And take a share with those that bear
   The budget and the apron!

"And by that stowp, my faith an' houpe,
   An' by that dear Kilbaigie!
If e'er ye want, or meet wi' scant,
   May I ne'er weet my craigie."
```

Cruikshank's caird is a noble creature; his face and figure show him to be fully capable of doing and saying all that is above written of him.

In the second part, the old tale of "The Three Hunchbacked Fiddlers" is illustrated with equal felicity. The famous classical dinners and duel in "Peregrine Pickle" are also excellent in their way; and the connoisseur of prints and etchings may see in the latter plate, and in another in this volume, how great the artist's mechanical skill is as an etcher. The distant view of the city in the duel, and of a market–place in "The Quack Doctor," are delightful specimens of the artist's skill in depicting buildings and backgrounds. They are touched with a grace, truth, and dexterity of workmanship that leave nothing to desire. We have before mentioned the man with the mouth, which appears in this number emblematical of gout and indigestion, in which the artist has shown all the fancy of Callot. Little demons, with long saws for noses, are making dreadful incisions into the toes of the unhappy sufferer; some are bringing pans of hot coals to keep the wounded member warm; a huge, solemn nightmare sits on the invalid's chest, staring solemnly into his eyes; a monster, with a pair of drumsticks, is banging a devil's tattoo on his forehead; and a pair of imps are nailing great tenpenny nails into his hands to make his happiness complete.

The late Mr. Clark's excellent work, "Three Courses and a Dessert," was published at a time when the rage for comic stories was not so great as it since has been, and Messrs. Clark and Cruikshank only sold their hundreds where Messrs. Dickens and Phiz dispose of their thousands. But if our recommendation can in any way influence the reader, we would enjoin him to have a copy of the "Three Courses," that contains some of the best designs of our artist, and some of the most amusing tales in our language. The invention of the pictures, for which Mr. Clark takes credit to himself, says a great deal for his wit and fancy. Can we, for instance, praise too highly the man who invented that wonderful oyster?

Examine him well; his beard, his pearl, his little round stomach, and his sweet smile. Only oysters know how to smile in this way; cool, gentle, waggish, and yet inexpressibly innocent and winning. Dando himself must have allowed such an artless native to go free, and consigned him to the glassy, cool, translucent wave again.

In writing upon such subjects as these with which we have been furnished, it can hardly be expected that we should follow any fixed plan and order—we must therefore take such advantage as we may, and seize upon our subject when and wherever we can lay hold of him.

For Jews, sailors, Irishmen, Hessian boots, little boys, beadles, policemen, tall life–guardsmen, charity children, pumps, dustmen, very short pantaloons, dandies in spectacles, and ladies with aquiline noses, remarkably taper waists, and wonderfully long ringlets, Mr. Cruikshank has a special predilection. The tribe of Israelites he has studied with amazing gusto; witness the Jew in Mr. Ainsworth's "Jack Sheppard," and the immortal Fagin of "Oliver Twist." Whereabouts lies the comic vis in these persons and things? Why should a beadle be comic, and his opposite a charity boy? Why should a tall life–guardsman have something in him essentially absurd? Why are short breeches more ridiculous than long? What is there particularly jocose about a pump, and wherefore does a long nose always provoke the beholder to laughter? These points may be metaphysically elucidated by those who list. It is probable that Mr. Cruikshank could not give an accurate definition of that which is ridiculous in these objects, but his instinct has told him that fun lurks in them, and cold must be the heart that can pass by the pantaloons of his charity boys, the Hessian boots of his dandies, and the fan–tail hats of his dustmen, without respectful wonder.

He has made a complete little gallery of dustmen. There is, in the first place, the professional dustman, who, having in the enthusiastic exercise of his delightful trade, laid hands upon property not strictly his own, is pursued, we presume, by the right owner, from whom he flies as fast as his crooked shanks will carry him.

George Cruikshank

What a curious picture it is—the horrid rickety houses in some dingy suburb of London, the grinning cobbler, the smothered butcher, the very trees which are covered with dust—it is fine to look at the different expressions of the two interesting fugitives. The fiery charioteer who belabors the poor donkey has still a glance for his brother on foot, on whom punishment is about to descend. And not a little curious is it to think of the creative power of the man who has arranged this little tale of low life. How logically it is conducted, how cleverly each one of the accessories is made to contribute to the effect of the whole. What a deal of thought and humor has the artist expended on this little block of wood; a large picture might have been painted out of the very same materials, which Mr. Cruikshank, out of his wondrous fund of merriment and observation, can afford to throw away upon a drawing not two inches long. From the practical dustmen we pass to those purely poetical. There are three of them who rise on clouds of their own raising, the very genii of the sack and shovel.

Is there no one to write a sonnet to these?—and yet a whole poem was written about Peter Bell the wagoner, a character by no means so poetic.

And lastly, we have the dustman in love: the honest fellow having seen a young beauty stepping out of a gin—shop on a Sunday morning, is pressing eagerly his suit.

Gin has furnished many subjects to Mr. Cruikshank, who labors in his own sound and hearty way to teach his countrymen the dangers of that drink. In the "Sketch—Book" is a plate upon the subject, remarkable for fancy and beauty of design; it is called the "Gin Juggernaut," and represents a hideous moving palace, with a reeking still at the roof and vast gin—barrels for wheels, under which unhappy millions are crushed to death. An immense black cloud of desolation covers over the country through which the gin monster has passed, dimly looming through the darkness whereof you see an agreeable prospect of gibbets with men dangling, burnt houses, The vast cloud comes sweeping on in the wake of this horrible body—crusher; and you see, by way of contrast, a distant, smiling, sunshiny tract of old English country, where gin as yet is not known. The allegory is as good, as earnest, and as fanciful as one of John Bunyan's, and we have often fancied there was a similarity between the men.

The render will examine the work called "My Sketch—Book" with not a little amusement, and may gather from it, as we fancy, a good deal of information regarding the character of the individual man, George Cruikshank: what points strike his eye as a painter; what move his anger or admiration as a moralist; what classes he seems most especially disposed to observe, and what to ridicule. There are quacks of all kinds, to whom he has a mortal hatred; quack dandies, who assume under his pencil, perhaps in his eye, the most grotesque appearance possible—their hats grow larger, their legs infinitely more crooked and lean; the tassels of their canes swell out to a most preposterous size; the tails of their coats dwindle away, and finish where coat–tails generally begin. Let us lay a wager that Cruikshank, a man of the people if ever there was one, heartily hates and despises these supercilious, swaggering young gentlemen; and his contempt is not a whit the less laudable because there may be tant soit peu of prejudice in it. It is right and wholesome to scorn dandies, as Nelson said it was to hate Frenchmen; in which sentiment (as we have before said) George Cruikshank undoubtedly shares. In the "Sunday in London,"* Monsieur the Chef is instructing a kitchen–maid how to compound some rascally French kickshaw or the other—a pretty scoundrel truly! with what an air he wears that nightcap of his, and shrugs his lank shoulders, and chatters, and ogles, and grins: they are all the same, these mounseers; there are other two fellows—morbleu! one is putting his dirty fingers into the saucepan; there are frogs cooking in it, no doubt; and just over some other dish of abomination, another dirty rascal is taking snuff! Never mind, the sauce won't be hurt by a few ingredients more or less. Three such fellows as these are not worth one Englishman, that's clear. There is one in the very midst of them, the great burly fellow with the beef: he could beat all three in five minutes. We cannot be certain that such was the process going on in Mr. Cruikshank's mind when he made the design; but some feelings of the sort were no doubt entertained by him.

* The following lines—ever fresh—by the author of "Headlong Hall," published years ago in the Globe and Traveller, are an excellent comment on several of the cuts from the "Sunday in London:"—

I.

"The poor man's sins are glaring;
  In the face of ghostly warning
    He is caught in the fact
    Of an overt act,
  Buying greens on Sunday morning.

II.

"The rich man's sins are hidden

16

George Cruikshank

```
In the pomp of wealth and station,
   And escape the sight
   Of the children of light,
Who are wise in their generation.

         III.

"The rich man has a kitchen,
And cooks to dress his dinner;
   The poor who would roast,
   To the baker's must post,
And thus becomes a sinner.

         IV.

"The rich man's painted windows
 Hide the concerts of the quality;
   The poor can but share
   A crack'd fiddle in the air,
Which offends all sound morality.

         V.

"The rich man has a cellar,
And a ready butler by him;
   The poor must steer
   For his pint of beer
Where the saint can't choose but spy him.

         VI.

"This rich man is invisible
 In the crowd of his gay society;
   But the poor man's delight
   Is a sore in the sight
And a stench in the nose of piety."
```

Against dandy footmen he is particularly severe. He hates idlers, pretenders, boasters, and punishes these fellows as best he may. Who does not recollect the famous picture, "What IS taxes, Thomas?" What is taxes indeed; well may that vast, over-fed, lounging flunky ask the question of his associate Thomas: and yet not well, for all that Thomas says in reply is, "I DON'T KNOW." "O beati PLUSHICOLAE," what a charming state of

17

ignorance is yours! In the "Sketch-Book" many footmen make their appearance: one is a huge fat Hercules of a Portman Square porter, who calmly surveys another poor fellow, a porter likewise, but out of livery, who comes staggering forward with a box that Hercules might lift with his little finger. Will Hercules do so? not he. The giant can carry nothing heavier than a cocked-hat note on a silver tray, and his labors are to walk from his sentry-box to the door, and from the door back to his sentry-box, and to read the Sunday paper, and to poke the hall fire twice or thrice, and to make five meals a day. Such a fellow does Cruikshank hate and scorn worse even than a Frenchman.

The man's master, too, comes in for no small share of our artist's wrath. There is a company of them at church, who humbly designate themselves "miserable sinners!" Miserable sinners indeed! Oh, what floods of turtle-soup, what tons of turbot and lobster-sauce must have been sacrificed to make those sinners properly miserable. My lady with the ermine tippet and draggling feather, can we not see that she lives in Portland Place, and is the wife of an East India Director? She has been to the Opera over-night (indeed her husband, on her right, with his fat hand dangling over the pew-door, is at this minute thinking of Mademoiselle Leocadie, whom he saw behind the scenes)—she has been at the Opera over-night, which with a trifle of supper afterwards—a white-and-brown soup, a lobster- salad, some woodcocks, and a little champagne—sent her to bed quite comfortable. At half-past eight her maid brings her chocolate in bed, at ten she has fresh eggs and muffins, with, perhaps, a half- hundred of prawns for breakfast, and so can get over the day and the sermon till lunch-time pretty well. What an odor of musk and bergamot exhales from the pew!—how it is wadded, and stuffed, and spangled over with brass nails! what hassocks are there for those who are not too fat to kneel! what a flustering and flapping of gilt prayer-books; and what a pious whirring of bible leaves one hears all over the church, as the doctor blandly gives out the text! To be miserable at this rate you must, at the very least, have four thousand a year: and many persons are there so enamored of grief and sin, that they would willingly take the risk of the misery to have a life-interest in the consols that accompany it, quite careless about consequences, and sceptical as to the notion that a day is at hand when you must fulfil YOUR SHARE OF THE BARGAIN.

Our artist loves to joke at a soldier; in whose livery there appears to him to be something almost as ridiculous as in the uniform of the gentleman of the shoulder-knot. Tall life-guardsmen and fierce grenadiers figure in many of his designs, and almost always in a ridiculous way. Here again we have the honest popular English feeling which jeers at pomp or pretension of all kinds, and is especially jealous of all display of military authority. "Raw Recruit," "ditto dressed," ditto "served up," as we see them in the "Sketch–Book," are so many satires upon the army: Hodge with his ribbons flaunting in his hat, or with red coat and musket, drilled stiff and pompous, or at last, minus leg and arm, tottering about on crutches, does not fill our English artist with the enthusiasm that follows the soldier in every other part of Europe. Jeanjean, the conscript in France, is laughed at to be sure, but then it is because he is a bad soldier: when he comes to have a huge pair of mustachios and the croix–d'honneur to briller on his poitrine cicatrisee, Jeanjean becomes a member of a class that is more respected than any other in the French nation. The veteran soldier inspires our people with no such awe—we hold that democratic weapon the fist in much more honor than the sabre and bayonet, and laugh at a man tricked out in scarlet and pipe–clay.

That regiment of heroes is "marching to divine service," to the tune of the "British Grenadiers." There they march in state, and a pretty contempt our artist shows for all their gimcracks and trumpery. He has drawn a perfectly English scene—the little blackguard boys are playing pranks round about the men, and shouting, "Heads up, soldier," "Eyes right, lobster," as little British urchins will do. Did one ever hear the like sentiments expressed in France? Shade of Napoleon, we insult you by asking the question. In England, however, see how different the case is: and designedly or undesignedly, the artist has opened to us a piece of his mind. In the crowd the only person who admires the soldiers is the poor idiot, whose pocket a rogue is picking. There is another picture, in which the sentiment is much the same, only, as in the former drawing we see Englishmen laughing at the troops of the line, here are Irishmen giggling at the militia.

We have said that our artist has a great love for the drolleries of the Green Island. Would any one doubt what was the country of the merry fellows depicted in his group of Paddies?

```
"Place me amid O'Rourkes, O'Tooles,
   The ragged royal race of Tara;
Or place me where Dick Martin rules
   The pathless wilds of Connemara."
```

We know not if Mr. Cruikshank has ever had any such good luck as to see the Irish in Ireland itself, but he certainly has obtained a knowledge of their looks, as if the country had been all his life familiar to him. Could Mr. O'Connell himself desire anything more national than the scene of a drunken row, or could Father Mathew have a better text to preach upon? There is not a broken nose in the room that is not thoroughly Irish.

We have then a couple of compositions treated in a graver manner, as characteristic too as the other. We call attention to the comical look of poor Teague, who has been pursued and beaten by the witch's stick, in order to point out also the singular neatness of the workmanship, and the pretty, fanciful little glimpse of landscape that the artist has introduced in the background. Mr. Cruikshank has a fine eye for such homely landscapes, and renders them with great delicacy and taste. Old villages, farm–yards, groups of stacks, queer chimneys, churches, gable–ended cottages, Elizabethan mansion–houses, and other old English scenes, he depicts with evident enthusiasm.

Famous books in their day were Cruikshank's "John Gilpin" and "Epping Hunt;" for though our artist does not draw horses very scientifically,—to use a phrase of the atelier,—he FEELS them very keenly; and his queer animals, after one is used to them, answer quite as well as better. Neither is he very happy in trees, and such rustical produce; or, rather, we should say, he is very original, his trees being decidedly of his own make and composition, not imitated from any master.

But what then? Can a man be supposed to imitate everything? We know what the noblest study of mankind is, and to this Mr. Cruikshank has confined himself. That postilion with the people in the broken–down chaise roaring after him is as deaf as the post by which he passes. Suppose all the accessories were away, could not one swear that the man was stone–deaf, beyond the reach of trumpet? What is the peculiar character in a deaf man's physiognomy?—can any person define it satisfactorily in words?—not in pages; and Mr. Cruikshank has expressed it on a piece of paper not so big as the tenth part of your thumb–nail. The horses of John Gilpin are much more of the equestrian order; and as here the artist has only his favorite suburban buildings to draw, not a word is to be said against his design. The inn and old buildings are charmingly designed, and nothing can be more prettily or playfully touched.

```
"At Edmonton his loving wife
   From the balcony spied
 Her tender husband, wond'ring much
   To see how he did ride.
```

George Cruikshank

```
"'Stop, stop, John Gilpin!  Here's the house!'
   They all at once did cry;
 'The dinner waits, and we are tired-'
   Said Gilpin-'So am I!'

"Six gentlemen upon the road
   Thus seeing Gilpin fly,
 With post-boy scamp'ring in the rear,
   They raised the hue and cry:-

"'Stop thief! stop thief!-a highwayman!'
   Not one of them was mute;
 And all and each that passed that way
   Did join in the pursuit.

"And now the turnpike gates again
   Flew open in short space;
 The toll-men thinking, as before,
   That Gilpin rode a race."
```

The rush, and shouting, and clatter are excellently depicted by the artist; and we, who have been scoffing at his manner of designing animals, must here make a special exception in favor of the hens and chickens; each has a different action, and is curiously natural.

Happy are children of all ages who have such a ballad and such pictures as this in store for them! It is a comfort to think that woodcuts never wear out, and that the book still may be had for a shilling, for those who can command that sum of money.

In the "Epping Hunt," which we owe to the facetious pen of Mr. Hood, our artist has not been so successful. There is here too much horsemanship and not enough incident for him; but the portrait of Roundings the huntsman is an excellent sketch, and a couple of the designs contain great humor. The first represents the Cockney hero, who, "like a bird, was singing out while sitting on a tree."

And in the second the natural order is reversed. The stag having taken heart, is hunting the huntsman, and the Cheapside Nimrod is most ignominiously running away.

The Easter Hunt, we are told, is no more; and as the Quarterly Review recommends the

British public to purchase Mr. Catlin's pictures, as they form the only record of an interesting race now rapidly passing away, in like manner we should exhort all our friends to purchase Mr. Cruikshank's designs of ANOTHER interesting race, that is run already and for the last time.

Besides these, we must mention, in the line of our duty, the notable tragedies of "Tom Thumb" and "Bombastes Furioso," both of which have appeared with many illustrations by Mr. Cruikshank. The "brave army" of Bombastes exhibits a terrific display of brutal force, which must shock the sensibilities of an English radical. And we can well understand the caution of the general, who bids this soldatesque effrenee to begone, and not to kick up a row.

Such a troop of lawless ruffians let loose upon a populous city would play sad havoc in it; and we fancy the massacres of Birmingham renewed, or at least of Badajoz, which, though not quite so dreadful, if we may believe his Grace the Duke of Wellington, as the former scenes of slaughter, were nevertheless severe enough: but we must not venture upon any ill-timed pleasantries in presence of the disturbed King Arthur and the awful ghost of Gaffer Thumb.

We are thus carried at once into the supernatural, and here we find Cruikshank reigning supreme. He has invented in his time a little comic pandemonium, peopled with the most droll, good-natured fiends possible. We have before us Chamisso's "Peter Schlemihl," with Cruikshank's designs translated into German, and gaining nothing by the change. The "Kinder und Hans-Maerchen" of Grimm are likewise ornamented with a frontispiece copied from that one which appeared to the amusing version of the English work. The books on Phrenology and Time have been imitated by the same nation; and even in France, whither reputation travels slower than to any country except China, we have seen copies of the works of George Cruikshank.

He in return has complimented the French by illustrating a couple of Lives of Napoleon, and the "Life in Paris" before mentioned. He has also made designs for Victor Hugo's "Hans of Iceland." Strange, wild etchings were those, on a strange, mad subject; not so good in our notion as the designs for the German books, the peculiar humor of which latter seemed to suit the artist exactly. There is a mixture of the awful and the ridiculous in these, which perpetually excites and keeps awake the reader's attention; the German writer and the English artist seem to have an entire faith in their subject. The reader, no doubt, remembers the awful passage in "Peter Schlemihl," where the little gentleman purchases the shadow of that hero—"Have the kindness, noble sir, to examine and try this bag." "He put his hand into his pocket, and drew thence a tolerably large bag of Cordovan leather, to which a couple of thongs were fixed. I took it from him, and immediately counted out ten gold pieces, and ten more, and ten more, and still other ten, whereupon I held out my hand to him. Done, said I, it is a bargain; you shall have my shadow for your bag. The bargain was concluded; he knelt down before me, and I saw him with a wonderful neatness take my shadow from head to foot, lightly lift it up from the grass, roll and fold it up neatly, and at last pocket it. He then rose up, bowed to me once more, and walked away again, disappearing behind the rose bushes. I don't know, but I thought I heard him laughing a little. I, however, kept fast hold of the bag. Everything around me was bright in the sun, and as yet I gave no thought to what I had done."

This marvellous event, narrated by Peter with such a faithful, circumstantial detail, is painted by Cruikshank in the most wonderful poetic way, with that happy mixture of the real and supernatural that makes the narrative so curious, and like truth. The sun is shining with the utmost brilliancy in a great quiet park or garden; there is a palace in the background, and a statue basking in the sun quite lonely and melancholy; there is a sun–dial, on which is a deep shadow, and in the front stands Peter Schlemihl, bag in hand: the old gentleman is down on his knees to him, and has just lifted off the ground the SHADOW OF ONE LEG; he is going to fold it back neatly, as one does the tails of a coat, and will stow it, without any creases or crumples, along with the other black garments that lie in that immense pocket of his. Cruikshank has designed all this as if he had a very serious belief in the story; he laughs, to be sure, but one fancies that he is a little frightened in his heart, in spite of all his fun and joking.

The German tales we have mentioned before. "The Prince riding on the Fox," "Hans in Luck," "The Fiddler and his Goose," "Heads off," are all drawings which, albeit not before us now, nor seen for ten years, remain indelibly fixed on the memory. "Heisst du etwa Rumpelstilzchen?" There sits the Queen on her throne, surrounded by grinning beef–eaters, and little Rumpelstiltskin stamps his foot through the floor in the excess of his tremendous despair. In one of these German tales, if we remember rightly, there is an account of a little orphan who is carried away by a pitying fairy for a term of seven years, and passing that period of sweet apprenticeship among the imps and sprites of fairy–land. Has our artist been among the same company, and brought back their portraits in his sketch– book? He is the only designer fairy–land has had. Callot's imps, for all their strangeness, are only of the earth earthy. Fuseli's fairies belong to the infernal regions; they are monstrous, lurid, and hideously melancholy. Mr. Cruikshank alone has had a true insight into the character of the "little people." They are something like men and women, and yet not flesh and blood; they are laughing and mischievous, but why we know not. Mr. Cruikshank, however, has had some dream or the other, or else a natural mysterious instinct (as the Seherinn of Prevorst had for beholding ghosts), or else some preternatural fairy revelation, which has made him acquainted with the looks and ways of the fantastical subjects of Oberon and Titania.

We have, unfortunately, no fairy portraits; but, on the other hand, can descend lower than fairy-land, and have seen some fine specimens of devils. One has already been raised, and the reader has seen him tempting a fat Dutch burgomaster, in an ancient gloomy market-place, such as George Cruikshank can draw as well as Mr. Prout, Mr. Nash, or any man living. There is our friend once more; our friend the burgomaster, in a highly excited state, and running as hard as his great legs will carry him, with our mutual enemy at his tail.

What are the bets; will that long-legged bondholder of a devil come up with the honest Dutchman? It serves him right: why did he put his name to stamped paper? And yet we should not wonder if some lucky chance should turn up in the burgomaster's favor, and his infernal creditor lose his labor; for one so proverbially cunning as yonder tall individual with the saucer eyes, it must be confessed that he has been very often outwitted.

There is, for instance, the case of "The Gentleman in Black," which has been illustrated by our artist. A young French gentleman, by name M. Desonge, who, having expended his patrimony in a variety of taverns and gaming-houses, was one day pondering upon the exhausted state of his finances, and utterly at a loss to think how he should provide means for future support, exclaimed, very naturally, "What the devil shall I do?" He had no sooner spoken than a GENTLEMAN IN BLACK made his appearance, whose authentic portrait Mr. Cruikshank has had the honor to paint. This gentleman produced a black-edged book out of a black bag, some black-edged papers tied up with black crape, and sitting down familiarly opposite M. Desonge, began conversing with him on the state of his affairs.

George Cruikshank

It is needless to state what was the result of the interview. M. Desonge was induced by the gentleman to sign his name to one of the black–edged papers, and found himself at the close of the conversation to be possessed of an unlimited command of capital. This arrangement completed, the Gentleman in Black posted (in an extraordinarily rapid manner) from Paris to London, there found a young English merchant in exactly the same situation in which M. Desonge had been, and concluded a bargain with the Briton of exactly the same nature.

The book goes on to relate how these young men spent the money so miraculously handed over to them, and how both, when the period drew near that was to witness the performance of THEIR part of the bargain, grew melancholy, wretched, nay, so absolutely dishonorable as to seek for every means of breaking through their agreement. The Englishman living in a country where the lawyers are more astute than any other lawyers in the world, took the advice of a Mr. Bagsby, of Lyon's Inn; whose name, as we cannot find it in the "Law List," we presume to be fictitious. Who could it be that was a match for the devil? Lord —— very likely; we shall not give his name, but let every reader of this Review fill up the blank according to his own fancy, and on comparing it with the copy purchased by his neighbors, he will find that fifteen out of twenty have written down the same honored name.

Well, the Gentleman in Black was anxious for the fulfilment of his bond. The parties met at Mr. Bagsby's chambers to consult, the Black Gentleman foolishly thinking that he could act as his own counsel, and fearing no attorney alive. But mark the superiority of British law, and see how the black pettifogger was defeated.

Mr. Bagsby simply stated that he would take the case into Chancery, and his antagonist, utterly humiliated and defeated, refused to move a step farther in the matter.

And now the French gentleman, M. Desonge, hearing of his friend's escape, became anxious to be free from his own rash engagements. He employed the same counsel who had been successful in the former instance, but the Gentleman in Black was a great deal wiser by this time, and whether M. Desonge escaped, or whether he is now in that extensive place which is paved with good intentions, we shall not say. Those who are anxious to know had better purchase the book wherein all these interesting matters are duly set down. There is one more diabolical picture in our budget, engraved by Mr. Thompson, the same dexterous artist who has rendered the former diableries so well.

George Cruikshank

We may mention Mr. Thompson's name as among the first of the engravers to whom Cruikshank's designs have been entrusted; and next to him (if we may be allowed to make such arbitrary distinctions) we may place Mr. Williams; and the reader is not possibly aware of the immense difficulties to be overcome in the rendering of these little sketches, which, traced by the designer in a few hours, require weeks' labor from the engraver. Mr. Cruikshank has not been educated in the regular schools of drawing (very luckily for him, as we think), and consequently has had to make a manner for himself, which is quite unlike that of any other draftsman. There is nothing in the least mechanical about it; to produce his particular effects he uses his own particular lines, which are queer, free, fantastical, and must be followed in all their infinite twists and vagaries by the careful tool of the engraver. Those three lovely heads, for instance, imagined out of the rinds of lemons, are worth examining, not so much for the jovial humor and wonderful variety of feature exhibited in these darling countenances as for the engraver's part of the work. See the infinite delicate cross−lines and hatchings which he is obliged to render; let him go, not a hair's breadth, but the hundredth part of a hair's breadth, beyond the given line, and the FEELING of it is ruined. He receives these little dots and specks, and fantastical quirks of the pencil, and cuts away with a little knife round each, not too much nor too little. Antonio's pound of flesh did not puzzle the Jew so much; and so well does the engraver succeed at last, that we never remember to have met with a single artist who did not vow that the wood−cutter had utterly ruined his design.

Of Messrs. Thompson and Williams we have spoken as the first engravers in point of rank; however, the regulations of professional precedence are certainly very difficult, and the rest of their brethren we shall not endeavor to class. Why should the artists who executed the cuts of the admirable "Three Courses" yield the pas to any one?

There, for instance, is an engraving by Mr. Landells, nearly as good in our opinion as the very best woodcut that ever was made after Cruikshank, and curiously happy in rendering the artist's peculiar manner: this cut does not come from the facetious publications which we have consulted; but is a contribution by Mr. Cruikshank to an elaborate and splendid botanical work upon the Orchidaceae of Mexico, by Mr. Bateman. Mr. Bateman despatched some extremely choice roots of this valuable plant to a friend in England, who, on the arrival of the case, consigned it to his gardener to unpack. A great deal of anxiety with regard to the contents was manifested by all concerned, but on the lid of the box being removed, there issued from it three or four fine specimens of the enormous Blatta beetle that had been preying upon the plants during the voyage; against these the gardeners, the grooms, the porters, and the porters' children, issued forth in arms, and this scene the artist has immortalized.

We have spoken of the admirable way in which Mr. Cruikshank has depicted Irish character and Cockney character; English country character is quite as faithfully delineated in the person of the stout porteress and her children, and of the "Chawbacon" with the shovel, on whose face is written "Zummerzetsheer." Chawbacon appears in another plate, or else Chawbacon's brother. He has come up to Lunnan, and is looking about him at raaces.

How distinct are these rustics from those whom we have just been examining! They hang about the purlieus of the metropolis: Brook Green, Epsom, Greenwich, Ascot, Goodwood, are their haunts. They visit London professionally once a year, and that is at the time of Bartholomew fair. How one may speculate upon the different degrees of rascality, as exhibited in each face of the thimblerigging trio, and form little histories for these worthies, charming Newgate romances, such as have been of late the fashion! Is any man so blind that he cannot see the exact face that is writhing under the thhnblerigged hero's hat? Like Timanthes of old, our artist expresses great passions without the aid of the human countenance. There is another specimen—a street row of inebriated bottles. Is there any need of having a face after this? "Come on!" says Claret-bottle, a dashing, genteel fellow, with his hat on one ear—"Come on! has any man a mind to tap me?" Claret-bottle is a little screwed (as one may see by his legs), but full of gayety and courage; not so that stout, apoplectic Bottle-of-rum, who has staggered against the wall, and has his hand upon his liver: the fellow hurts himself with smoking, that is clear, and is as sick as sick can be. See, Port is making away from the storm, and Double X is as flat as ditch-water. Against these, awful in their white robes, the sober watchmen come.

Our artist then can cover up faces, and yet show them quite clearly, as in the thimblerig group; or he can do without faces altogether; or he can, at a pinch, provide a countenance for a gentleman out of any given object—a beautiful Irish physiognomy being moulded upon a keg of whiskey; and a jolly English countenance frothing out of a pot of ale (the spirit of brave Toby Philpot come back to reanimate his clay); while in a fungus may be recognized the physiognomy of a mushroom peer. Finally, if he is at a loss, he can make a living head, body, and legs out of steel or tortoise-shell, as in the case of the vivacious pair of spectacles that are jockeying the nose of Caddy Cuddle.

George Cruikshank

Of late years Mr. Cruikshank has busied himself very much with steel engraving, and the consequences of that lucky invention have been, that his plates are now sold by thousands, where they could only be produced by hundreds before. He has made many a bookseller's and author's fortune (we trust that in so doing he may not have neglected his own). Twelve admirable plates, furnished yearly to that facetious little publication, the Comic Almanac, have gained for it a sale, as we hear, of nearly twenty thousand copies. The idea of the work was novel; there was, in the first number especially, a great deal of comic power, and Cruikshank's designs were so admirable that the Almanac at once became a vast favorite with the public, and has so remained ever since.

Besides the twelve plates, this almanac contains a prophetic woodcut, accompanying an awful Blarneyhum Astrologicum that appears in this and other almanacs. There is one that hints in pretty clear terms that with the Reform of Municipal Corporations the ruin of the great Lord Mayor of London is at hand. His lordship is meekly going to dine at an eightpenny ordinary, his giants in pawn, his men in armor dwindled to "one poor knight," his carriage to be sold, his stalwart aldermen vanished, his sheriffs, alas! and alas! in gaol! Another design shows that Rigdum, if a true, is also a moral and instructive prophet. John Bull is asleep, or rather in a vision; the cunning demon, Speculation, blowing a thousand bright bubbles about him. Meanwhile the rooks are busy at his fob, a knave has cut a cruel hole in his pocket, a rattlesnake has coiled safe round his feet, and will in a trice swallow Bull, chair, money and all; the rats are at his corn−bags (as if, poor devil, he had corn to spare); his faithful dog is bolting his leg−of−mutton—nay, a thief has gotten hold of his very candle, and there, by way of moral, is his ale−pot, which looks and winks in his face, and seems to say, O Bull, all this is froth, and a cruel satirical picture of a certain rustic who had a goose that laid certain golden eggs, which goose the rustic slew in expectation of finding all the eggs at once. This is goose and sage too, to borrow the pun of "learned Doctor Gill;" but we shrewdly suspect that Mr. Cruikshank is becoming a little conservative in his notions.

We love these pictures so that it is hard to part us, and we still fondly endeavor to hold on, but this wild word, farewell, must be spoken by the best friends at last, and so good−by, brave woodcuts: we feel quite a sadness in coming to the last of our collection.

In the earlier numbers of the Comic Almanac all the manners and customs of Londoners that would afford food for fun were noted down; and if during the last two years the mysterious personage who, under the title of "Rigdum Funnidos," compiles this ephemeris, has been compelled to resort to romantic tales, we must suppose that he did so because the great metropolis was exhausted, and it was necessary to discover new worlds in the cloud–land of fancy. The character of Mr. Stubbs, who made his appearance in the Almanac for 1839, had, we think, great merit, although his adventures were somewhat of too tragical a description to provoke pure laughter.

We should be glad to devote a few pages to the "Illustratons of Time," the "Scraps and Sketches," and the "Illustrations of Phrenology," which are among the most famous of our artist's publications; but it is very difficult to find new terms of praise, as find them one must, when reviewing Mr. Cruikshank's publications, and more difficult still (as the reader of this notice will no doubt have perceived for himself long since) to translate his design into words, and go to the printer's box for a description of all that fun and humor which the artist can produce by a few skilful turns of his needle. A famous article upon the "Illustrations of Time" appeared some dozen years since in Blackwood's Magazine, of which the conductors have always been great admirers of our artist, as became men of honor and genius. To these grand qualities do not let it be supposed that we are laying claim, but, thank heaven, Cruikshank's humor is so good and benevolent that any man must love it, and on this score we may speak as well as another.

Then there are the "Greenwich Hospital" designs, which must not be passed over. "Greenwich Hospital" is a hearty, good–natured book, in the Tom Dibdin school, treating of the virtues of British tars, in approved nautical language. They maul Frenchmen and Spaniards, they go out in brigs and take frigates, they relieve women in distress, and are yard–arm and yard–arming, athwart–hawsing, marlinspiking, binnacling, and helm's–a–leeing, as honest seamen invariably do, in novels, on the stage, and doubtless on board ship. This we cannot take upon us to say, but the artist, like a true Englishman, as he is, loves dearly these brave guardians of Old England, and chronicles their rare or fanciful exploits with the greatest good–will. Let any one look at the noble head of Nelson in the "Family Library," and they will, we are sure, think with us that the designer must have felt and loved what he drew. There are to this abridgment of Southey's admirable book many more cuts after Cruikshank; and about a dozen pieces by the same hand will be found in a work equally popular, Lockhart's excellent "Life of Napoleon." Among these the retreat from Moscow is very fine; the Mamlouks most vigorous, furious, and barbarous, as they should be. At the end of these three volumes Mr. Cruikshank's contributions to the "Family Library" seem suddenly to have ceased.

George Cruikshank

We are not at all disposed to undervalue the works and genius of Mr. Dickens, and we are sure that he would admit as readily as any man the wonderful assistance that he has derived from the artist who has given us the portraits of his ideal personages, and made them familiar to all the world. Once seen, these figures remain impressed on the memory, which otherwise would have had no hold upon them, and the heroes and heroines of Boz become personal acquaintances with each of us. Oh, that Hogarth could have illustrated Fielding in the same way! and fixed down on paper those grand figures of Parson Adams, and Squire Allworthy, and the great Jonathan Wild.

With regard to the modern romance of "Jack Sheppard," in which the latter personage makes a second appearance, it seems to us that Mr. Cruikshank really created the tale, and that Mr. Ainsworth, as it were, only put words to it. Let any reader of the novel think over it for a while, now that it is some months since he has perused and laid it down—let him think, and tell us what he remembers of the tale? George Cruikshank's pictures—always George Cruikshank's pictures. The storm in the Thames, for instance: all the author's labored description of that event has passed clean away—we have only before the mind's eye the fine plates of Cruikshank: the poor wretch cowering under the bridge arch, as the waves come rushing in, and the boats are whirling away in the drift of the great swollen black waters. And let any man look at that second plate of the murder on the Thames, and he must acknowledge how much more brilliant the artist's description is than the writer's, and what a real genius for the terrible as well as for the ridiculous the former has; how awful is the gloom of the old bridge, a few lights glimmering from the houses here and there, but not so as to be reflected on the water at all, which is too turbid and raging: a great heavy rack of clouds goes sweeping over the bridge, and men with flaring torches, the murderers, are borne away with the stream.

The author requires many pages to describe the fury of the storm, which Mr. Cruikshank has represented in one. First, he has to prepare you with the something inexpressibly melancholy in sailing on a dark night upon the Thames: "the ripple of the water," "the darkling current," "the indistinctively seen craft," "the solemn shadows" and other phenomena visible on rivers at night are detailed (with not unskilful rhetoric) in order to bring the reader into a proper frame of mind for the deeper gloom and horror which is to ensue. Then follow pages of description. "As Rowland sprang to the helm, and gave the signal for pursuit, a war like a volley of ordnance was heard aloft, and the wind again burst its bondage. A moment before the surface of the stream was as black as ink. It was now whitening, hissing, and seething, like an enormous caldron. The blast once more swept over the agitated river, whirled off the sheets of foam, scattered them far and wide in rain–drops, and left the raging torrent blacker than before. Destruction everywhere marked the course of the gale. Steeples toppled and towers reeled beneath its fury. All was darkness, horror, confusion, ruin. Men fled from their tottering habitations and returned to them, scared by greater danger. The end of the world seemed at hand. . . . The hurricane had now reached its climax. The blast shrieked, as if exulting in its wrathful mission. Stunning and continuous, the din seemed almost to take away the power of hearing. He who had faced the gale WOULD HAVE BEEN INSTANTLY STIFLED," See with what a tremendous war of words (and good loud words too; Mr. Ainsworth's description is a good and spirited one) the author is obliged to pour in upon the reader before he can effect his purpose upon the latter, and inspire him with a proper terror. The painter does it at a glance, and old Wood's dilemma in the midst of that tremendous storm, with the little infant at his bosom, is remembered afterwards, not from the words, but from the visible image of them that the artist has left us.

It would not, perhaps, be out of place to glance through the whole of the "Jack Sheppard" plates, which are among the most finished and the most successful of Mr. Cruikshank's performances, and say a word or two concerning them. Let us begin with finding fault with No. 1, "Mr. Wood offers to adopt little Jack Sheppard." A poor print, on a poor subject; the figure of the woman not as carefully designed as it might be, and the expression of the eyes (not an uncommon fault with our artist) much caricatured. The print is cut up, to use the artist's phrase, by the number of accessories which the engraver has thought proper, after the author's elaborate description, elaborately to reproduce. The plate of "Wild discovering Darrell in the loft" is admirable—ghastly, terrible, and the treatment of it extraordinarily skilful, minute, and bold. The intricacies of the tile–work, and the mysterious twinkling of light among the beams, are excellently felt and rendered; and one sees here, as in the two next plates of the storm and murder, what a fine eye the artist has, what a skilful hand, and what a sympathy for the wild and dreadful. As a mere imitation of nature, the clouds and the bridge in the murder picture may be examined by painters who make far higher pretensions than Mr. Cruikshank. In point of workmanship they are equally good, the manner quite unaffected, the effect produced without any violent contrast, the whole scene evidently well and philosophically arranged in the artist's brain, before he began to put it upon copper.

The famous drawing of "Jack carving the name on the beam," which has been transferred to half the play–bills in town, is overloaded with accessories, as the first plate; but they are much better arranged than in the last–named engraving, and do not injure the effect of the principal figure. Remark, too, the conscientiousness of the artist, and that shrewd pervading idea of FORM which is one of his principal characteristics. Jack is surrounded by all sorts of implements of his profession; he stands on a regular carpenter's table: away in the shadow under it lie shavings and a couple of carpenter's hampers. The glue–pot, the mallet, the chisel–handle, the planes, the saws, the hone with its cover, and the other paraphernalia are all represented with extraordinary accuracy and forethought. The man's mind has retained the exact DRAWING of all these minute objects (unconsciously perhaps to himself), but we can see with what keen eyes he must go through the world, and what a fund of facts (as such a knowledge of the shape of objects is in his profession) this keen student of nature has stored away in his brain. In the next plate, where Jack is escaping from his mistress, the figure of that lady, one of the deepest of the [Greek text omitted], strikes us as disagreeable and unrefined; that of Winifred is, on the contrary, very pretty and graceful; and Jack's puzzled, slinking look must not be forgotten. All the accessories are good, and the apartment has a snug, cosy air; which is not remarkable, except that it shows how faithfully the designer has performed his work, and how curiously he has entered into all the particulars of the subject.

Master Thames Darrell, the handsome young man of the book, is, in Mr. Cruikshank's portraits of him, no favorite of ours. The lad seems to wish to make up for the natural insignificance of his face by frowning on all occasions most portentously. This figure, borrowed from the compositor's desk, will give a notion of what we mean. Wild's face is too violent for the great man of history (if we may call Fielding history), but this is in consonance with the ranting, frowning, braggadocio character that Mr. Ainsworth has given him.

The "Interior of Willesden Church" is excellent as a composition, and a piece of artistical workmanship; the groups are well arranged; and the figure of Mrs. Sheppard looking round alarmed, as her son is robbing the dandy Kneebone, is charming, simple, and unaffected. Not so "Mrs. Sheppard ill in bed," whose face is screwed up to an expression vastly too tragic. The little glimpse of the church seen through the open door of the room is very beautiful and poetical: it is in such small hints that an artist especially excels; they are the morals which he loves to append to his stories, and are always appropriate and welcome. The boozing ken is not to our liking; Mrs. Sheppard is there with her horrified eyebrows again. Why this exaggeration—is it necessary for the public? We think not, or if they require such excitement, let our artist, like a true painter as he is, teach them better things.*

* A gentleman (whose wit is so celebrated that one should be very cautious in repeating his stories) gave the writer a good illustration of the philosophy of exaggeration. Mr. —— was once behind the scenes at the Opera when the scene–shifters were preparing for the ballet. Flora was to sleep under a bush, whereon were growing a number of roses, and amidst which was fluttering a gay covey of butterflies. In size the roses exceeded the most expansive sunflowers, and the butterflies were as large as cocked hats;—the scene–shifter explained to Mr. ——, who asked the reason why everything was so magnified, that the galleries could never see the objects unless they were enormously exaggerated. How many of our writers and designers work for the galleries?

The "Escape from Willesden Cage" is excellent; the "Burglary in Wood's house" has not less merit; "Mrs. Sheppard in Bedlam," a ghastly picture indeed, is finely conceived, but not, as we fancy, so carefully executed; it would be better for a little more careful drawing in the female figure.

"Jack sitting for his picture" is a very pleasing group, and savors of the manner of Hogarth, who is introduced in the company. The "Murder of Trenchard" must be noticed too as remarkable for the effect and terrible vigor which the artist has given to the scene. The "Willesden Churchyard" has great merit too, but the gems of the book are the little vignettes illustrating the escape from Newgate. Here, too, much anatomical care of drawing is not required; the figures are so small that the outline and attitude need only to be indicated, and the designer has produced a series of figures quite remarkable for reality and poetry too. There are no less than ten of Jack's feats so described by Mr. Cruikshank. (Let us say a word here in praise of the excellent manner in which the author has carried us through the adventure.) Here is Jack clattering up the chimney, now peering into the lonely red room, now opening "the door between the red room and the chapel." What a wild, fierce, scared look he has, the young ruffian, as cautiously he steps in, holding light his bar of iron. You can see by his face how his heart is beating! If any one were there! but no! And this is a very fine characteristic of the prints, the extreme LONELINESS of them all. Not a soul is there to disturb him—woe to him who should—and Jack drives in the chapel gate, and shatters down the passage door, and there you have him on the leads. Up he goes! it is but a spring of a few feet from the blanket, and he is gone—abiit, evasit, erupit! Mr. Wild must catch him again if he can.

George Cruikshank

We must not forget to mention "Oliver Twist," and Mr. Cruikshank's famous designs to that work.* The sausage scene at Fagin's, Nancy seizing the boy; that capital piece of humor, Mr. Bumble's courtship, which is even better in Cruikshank's version than in Boz's exquisite account of the interview; Sykes's farewell to the dog; and the Jew,—the dreadful Jew—that Cruikshank drew! What a fine touching picture of melancholy desolation is that of Sykes and the dog! The poor cur is not too well drawn, the landscape is stiff and formal; but in this case the faults, if faults they be, of execution rather add to than diminish the effect of the picture: it has a strange, wild, dreary, broken–hearted look; we fancy we see the landscape as it must have appeared to Sykes, when ghastly and with bloodshot eyes he looked at it. As for the Jew in the dungeon, let us say nothing of it—what can we say to describe it? What a fine homely poet is the man who can produce this little world of mirth or woe for us! Does he elaborate his effects by slow process of thought, or do they come to him by instinct? Does the painter ever arrange in his brain an image so complete, that he afterwards can copy it exactly on the canvas, or does the hand work in spite of him?

* Or his new work, "The Tower of London," which promises even to surpass Mr. Cruikshank's former productions.

A great deal of this random work of course every artist has done in his time; many men produce effects of which they never dreamed, and strike off excellences, haphazard, which gain for them reputation; but a fine quality in Mr. Cruikshank, the quality of his success, as we have said before, is the extraordinary earnestness and good faith with which he executes all he attempts—the ludicrous, the polite, the low, the terrible. In the second of these he often, in our fancy, fails, his figures lacking elegance and descending to caricature; but there is something fine in this too: it is good that he SHOULD fail, that he should have these honest naive notions regarding the beau monde, the characteristics of which a namby–pamby tea–party painter could hit off far better than he. He is a great deal too downright and manly to appreciate the flimsy delicacies of small society—you cannot expect a lion to roar you like any sucking dove, or frisk about a drawing–room like a lady's little spaniel.

If then, in the course of his life and business, he has been occasionally obliged to imitate the ways of such small animals, he has done so, let us say it at once, clumsily, and like as a lion should. Many artists, we hear, hold his works rather cheap; they prate about bad drawing, want of scientific knowledge:—they would have something vastly more neat,

34

George Cruikshank

regular, anatomical.

Not one of the whole band most likely but can paint an Academy figure better than himself; nay, or a portrait of an alderman's lady and family of children. But look down the list of the painters and tell us who are they? How many among these men are POETS (makers), possessing the faculty to create, the greatest among the gifts with which Providence has endowed the mind of man? Say how many there are, count up what they have done, and see what in the course of some nine–and–twenty years has been done by this indefatigable man.

What amazing energetic fecundity do we find in him! As a boy he began to fight for bread, has been hungry (twice a day we trust) ever since, and has been obliged to sell his wit for his bread week by week. And his wit, sterling gold as it is, will find no such purchasers as the fashionable painter's thin pinchbeck, who can live comfortably for six weeks, when paid for and painting a portrait, and fancies his mind prodigiously occupied all the while. There was an artist in Paris, an artist hairdresser, who used to be fatigued and take restoratives after inventing a new coiffure. By no such gentle operation of head–dressing has Cruikshank lived: time was (we are told so in print) when for a picture with thirty heads in it he was paid three guineas—a poor week's pittance truly, and a dire week's labor. We make no doubt that the same labor would at present bring him twenty times the sum; but whether it be ill paid or well, what labor has Mr. Cruikshank's been! Week by week, for thirty years, to produce something new; some smiling offspring of painful labor, quite independent and distinct from its ten thousand jovial brethren; in what hours of sorrow and ill–health to be told by the world, "Make us laugh or you starve—Give us fresh fun; we have eaten up the old and are hungry. And all this has he been obliged to do—to wring laughter day by day, sometimes, perhaps, out of want, often certainly from ill–health or depression—to keep the fire of his brain perpetually alight: for the greedy public will give it no leisure to cool. This he has done and done well. He has told a thousand truths in as many strange and fascinating ways; he has given a thousand new and pleasant thoughts to millions of people; he has never used his wit dishonestly; he has never, in all the exuberance of his frolicsome humor, caused a single painful or guilty blush: how little do we think of the extraordinary power of this man, and how ungrateful we are to him!

Here, as we are come round to the charge of ingratitude, the starting–post from which we set out, perhaps we had better conclude. The reader will perhaps wonder at the high–flown tone in which we speak of the services and merits of an individual, whom he considers a humble scraper on steel, that is wonderfully popular already. But none of us remember all the benefits we owe him; they have come one by one, one driving out the memory of the other: it is only when we come to examine them all together, as the writer has done, who has a pile of books on the table before him—a heap of personal kindnesses from George Cruikshank (not presents, if you please, for we bought, borrowed, or stole every one of them)—that we feel what we owe him. Look at one of Mr. Cruikshank's works, and we pronounce him an excellent humorist. Look at all: his reputation is increased by a kind of geometrical progression; as a whole diamond is a hundred times more valuable than the hundred splinters into which it might be broken would be. A fine rough English diamond is this about which we have been writing.

Printed in the United Kingdom
by Lightning Source UK Ltd.
103616UKS00002BB/2